Harry the Haples

Written by Tonya Meers and Natasha Dennis
Illustrated by Chantal Bourgonje

Early Years Edition

1

First published in Great Britain in 2012 by Little Creative Days Ltd
Reprinted 2013

Copyright © Little Creative Days Ltd

ISBN 978-1-909875-07-4

This is a work of fiction. Names, characters, places, brands, media and incidents are either the product of the authors' imagination or are used fictitiously.

To our family for all their support and Sam for being our inspiration.

Harry the ghost, floated about in the bedroom upstairs.

"Right," he said, "I'm going to do it this time, just you watch me."

His brother Barry just rolled his eyes and sighed, "I'll believe it when I see it Harry, you're hopeless, all ghosts can float through walls, I don't know why you can't."

Harry took a deep breath and charged at the wall...thud!

"Ouch," Harry slid down the wall and ended up in a crumpled heap on the floor.
"I know I'm hopeless!" he sighed.
"I think you're trying too hard Harry, why don't you give up for today.
I know let's go and see what Wanda is cooking up, something nasty no doubt. She doesn't know how to be nice that one."

"Hubble bubble, toil and trouble this spell will turn that cat to rubble."
Flash. Bang.
'Meow' went the cat.
"Oh curses," muttered Wanda.
"I see you are still struggling to get a spell to work Wanda," said Harry as he and Barry floated into the lounge.
"Pesky cat won't sit still long enough for me to try my spells out on her."

"I'm not surprised," said Harry, "the last time you cast a spell on her it took 6 months for her to get her tail back."
"Why can't you do something nice for a change Wanda?" said Barry, "no wonder no-one likes you!"
"I'm not supposed to be nice; I'm a witch in case you hadn't noticed."

Meanwhile, Peter and Lucy, who were visiting their Gran, decided to go and explore the wood at the bottom of her garden.

"C'mon Lucy, let's go and see what we can find in the woods, we might even find that house that's supposed to be haunted."

"But what if it is haunted, Peter, we might not get back."

"Of course we will, there are no such things as ghosts and witches, they are just made up for Halloween to scare us kids."

So, off they went, through their Gran's back gate and down the pebbled path into the wood.

"C'mon Lucy, let's have a game of hide and seek."

"Ok, I'll count to 10 and you go and hide," said Lucy.

Peter looked for somewhere to hide and found a den that someone had already made. "I know, I'll hide in here," he said to himself, "Lucy will never find me!" Peter sat there for a few minutes and listened for Lucy, he heard her shouting his name in the distance. "Crikey," he said to himself, she's gone a long way; she must have gone off in a different direction. I better go and find her or she'll get lost and then we'll both be in trouble."

Peter eventually found Lucy.

"Do you know where we are Peter?"
"No, I've been so worried looking for you that I forgot to take a note of where I was going."
"Look Peter, there's a house over there with smoke coming out of the chimney,

so someone must be home."

Peter and Lucy looked at each other and gulped. "Crikey I think this must be the house that people say is haunted Lucy."

"It does look like it, what shall we do Peter?"

"Let's hide behind this tree and see if anyone goes in or out," said Peter.

"All I can see is a little old lady in the house. I'm feeling thirsty so why don't we go and ask for a glass of water."

"Ok Lucy. So much for this place being haunted, what a load of rubbish!" muttered Peter. Lucy and Peter knocked on the door.

They waited for an answer but no-one came. They knocked again but still no answer.

"Perhaps there wasn't anyone home after all," said Lucy.

"But we both saw that old woman." Peter decided to try the handle and the door creaked open.

"Hello," called Peter, "well the fire's going, look at that big pot of water bubbling away," said Lucy. Both children crept into the house and had a look around.
Harry and Barry hid behind the sofa, "We've got to get them out of here," whispered Harry, "Wanda is likely to turn them into toads if she catches them, you know what she's like. She's not fond of children!"
"What was that?" whispered Lucy.
"What?" said Peter.
"I thought I heard voices."
"I didn't hear anything."
"C'mon," said Harry; we need to get them out of here."
With that, Harry and Barry popped up from behind the sofa. Peter and Lucy jumped a foot in the air, screamed, and hid behind the chair.
"Ssh," said Harry, "Wanda will hear you."

Peter and Lucy peeped out from behind
the chair.
"Bbbbut you're ghosts," said Peter,
shaking.
"We know," said Barry, "but it's ok, we're
friendly ghosts and we won't hurt you."

With that, Harry and Barry gave them
both a big friendly smile.
"But I didn't think there were such a thing
as ghosts," said Peter.
"Well now you know there are!" said
Barry. "But we really need to get
you two out of here though as Wanda is

out the back chopping wood and she isn't so friendly."

"Who's Wanda?" asked Lucy.

"Wanda is a wicked witch," Barry replied. "We keep telling her to be nice so she will have more friends and her spells might work properly, but she just can't seem to do it!"

Just as Barry said that in walked Wanda carrying a large pile of wood.

"Well what have we got here boys?" she cackled "just what I needed for my spell, a couple of children."

Peter and Lucy started to edge back towards the door to leave but it suddenly slammed shut behind them and the bolt locked.

"Oh no you don't," cackled Wanda.

15

"Now come on Wanda, be nice to them, they haven't done you any harm," said Barry.

"Oh what's the point in being nice? Where will that get me? Witches aren't supposed to be nice!" exclaimed Wanda.

"It's ok Barry, she won't be able to do anything I've hidden her wand," whispered Harry.

"I heard that Harry, what have you done with it?" said Wanda.

Peter and Lucy both tried to get out of the door but it was locked and wouldn't open.

"What are we going to do now?" cried Lucy.

"Leave it to me," whispered Harry.

"Hey Wanda, is this what you're looking for?" Harry waved Wanda's wand about in the air.

"Give me that you over-sized

handkerchief."

"Oops," said Harry, who dropped the wand.

"Aha, got it," exclaimed Wanda.

"Now then you snivelling little toads, come here," said Wanda menacingly.

Peter and Lucy cowered behind the sofa as they saw the first flash just above them. Each time Wanda tried to crack the wand she just missed them. Harry and Barry tried to wrestle the wand from her but she was too quick for them. Then Harry charged at Wanda, he went straight through her and instead of his usual thud against the wall, he suddenly found himself outside.

"How did that happen?" Harry said to himself, "I guess Barry was right, I was trying too hard, I wasn't thinking about it and it worked. Better go and save those kids though before Wanda turns them into toads."

Too late. When Harry floated back into the room Peter and Lucy were bouncing around the floor croaking.
"Oh no, I'm so sorry kids," said Harry. "Wanda, why did you have to do that, they weren't harming anyone," said Harry. "Because I need a couple of toads for my spell," said Wanda triumphantly.

"But Wanda, your spells never work because you never want to do anything nice with them," said Barry, "so why don't you turn these two back into children and do something nice for a change."
Wanda knew Harry and Barry were right, nothing ever went right for her so she thought she would try it their way instead and with that she turned them both back

into children again.

Peter and Lucy were not sure what had just happened to them but they soon realised that Harry and Barry were quite friendly really.

Wanda cast a spell on some dead flowers in a vase and they turned into fresh ones. She knew then that Harry and Barry had been right all along so, in future all her spells would be nice ones.

Her next spell was to magic up some lovely cakes and lemonade and they all sat down to eat.

"Well," said Harry, "Wanda's finally cast a spell that works and I can now float through walls, look," and he floated in and out without a single thud!

THE END